The Adventures of Jo and Baby Brother

Spencer's Special Gift

by Tiffany Elle Burgess

Illustrated by TeMika Grooms

Published in 2019 by Tiffany Elle Burgess
Printed in the United States of America

ISBN 978-0-9978420-2-9

Written by Tiffany Elle Burgess, Illustrated by TeMika Grooms
Book Design by TeMika Grooms

www.tiffanyelleburgess.com

DEDICATION

This book is dedicated to my three older brothers, Francis, Jr., Matthew,

and Martin, and my four nephews.

I love you all!

-Tiffany Elle Burgess

Meet Spencer Bean, Jr. His family calls him, "Junior", for short. Spencer lives with his parents, Elizabeth-Jean and Spencer Bean, Sr. For four and a half years he has enjoyed all of his parents' attention, and just about anything he has ever wanted, he has gotten. Little Spencer's life has been quite easy breezy, that is, until the day he got an unforgettable gift from his parents. That was the day his life changed forever.

It all began one fall afternoon when Spencer's parents came home with a present for him. His mother walked through the front door of their blue and white brick home carrying a small yellow blanket, and underneath was Spencer's very special gift.

"We're home!" yelled Spencer's mother as she walked into the house.

"Junior!" his father called. "Come and see your baby brother!"

Spencer's father dropped all of the stuff he had in his hands—balloons, blue lollipops, and a suitcase—and opened his arms wide for Spencer to climb into them. Spencer ran from the kitchen, where he had been helping his Aunt Lynn bake cookies, and jumped into his father's arms. His Aunt Lynn, who had been babysitting him while his parents were off picking up his little brother, came running, too.

"Let me see. Let me see!" Spencer begged while tugging at the blanket.

"Okay, okay. Calm down, Junior," his mother instructed as she pulled back the blanket. "This is your brother, Matthew," she said.

"Eww!" squealed Spencer. "He looks funny, Mommy!"

Realizing what he had said, he cupped his hands over his mouth and quickly told his mother he was sorry. Spencer's mother laughed and explained to him that Matthew would not look like a tiny baby for long.

"Soon enough," she began, "Your baby brother will get bigger and bigger, as big as you even, and he will start to look different, too."

Hmm, Spencer thought to himself, *he will never be as big as me, I'm the big brother!*

For the rest of the day, Spencer helped his parents take care of Matthew. He helped his mother unpack Matthew's things, his clothes and toys, and place them in his new little brother's dresser drawers. After he finished, he spent time getting to know Matthew. He went into his parents' room and stared at his little brother as he was sleeping in his bassinet.

"Mattoo, Mattoo," he called. He listened to himself say Matthew a few more times and it still did not sound quite right to little Spencer. So he thought to himself, what can I call you? He thought, and thought, and thought. Then he smiled at Matthew and said, "I know! I'll call you, Baby, Baby Brotha'!"

Still excited about his special gift, Spencer counted Matthew's tiny fingers and toes, sang to his little brother, and played with his hair. Matthew continued to sleep and after a while, Spencer grew bored with his baby brother and began to look for something else to do.

He turned to his mother, "Mommy, can we play my Choo-Choo Chippy game?"

Choo-Choo Chippy was Spencer's favorite television character. Chippy was a chipmunk who rode a train around the world. Every day Chippy went on a new adventure. Spencer loved Choo-Choo Chippy. He had Choo-Choo Chippy socks, slippers, a toothbrush, blanket, and a board game. And he always won when he played the board game with his parents.

"Not now, Honey," his mother said, "I really need to get some rest. Ask your daddy to play with you."

This was new for Spencer. For four years, he got just about everything he wanted, including playing his favorite board game with his parents whenever he asked but he did as he was told and went to find his dad.

"Daddy!" Spencer yelled. "Will you play Choo-Choo Chippy with me, pleeease?" he begged.

"Oh, I can't right now, Son. I need to fix your old rocking chair for Matthew and Mommy. Why don't you ask your Aunt Lynn to play with you?"

Hmm, Spencer thought to himself again, why is everyone so busy with Matthew? He's not doing anything but sleeping. I can do a lot of things! I can talk and walk. I can play. I can sing and dance.

So Spencer went to find his Aunt Lynn, who was packing her suitcase, and started to sing the Choo-Choo Chippy theme song. His Aunt Lynn clapped while he sang and danced and Spencer got the attention he wanted, but it didn't last very long.

"Do you want to play my game with me, Aunt Lynn?" he asked.

"Now that your mommy, daddy, and Matthew are home, June bug, I'm going to my house. I'll be back to visit you all this weekend. We'll play Choo-Choo Chippy then, okay?"

Spencer was annoyed. Matthew had just gotten home and he was already changing things for him. He didn't like it one bit. After all, he was prepared for a new little brother, as prepared as a four-year-old boy could be....... or was he?

Over the next few weeks, Spencer noticed that his parents sure paid a lot of attention to Matthew, so much attention that they sometimes forgot about the little things that meant something to him. Before they brought his new baby brother home, they always remembered the little things. One week in particular, Spencer's parents seemed to forget everything!

On Tuesday morning, his mother was so busy calming down his crying baby brother that she forgot to sing the "See You Later, Alligator" song to him before he left for preschool. That was his favorite song and she always sang it to him. Spencer stood by the door waiting for her to start singing.

"Come on, Junior, let's go. We're running late," said his father as he grabbed his car keys and Spencer's back pack.

"Ok, Daddy," Spencer replied. "Bye, Mommy," he said walking as slowly as he could out of the front door.

"Bye, Sweetheart," she replied. "Have a good day at school," she said. But still no song.

On Wednesday, Spencer's dad forgot to give him extra money for a snack. Wednesdays were "Snack Day" at Spencer's preschool and each child got to buy a treat at lunch time. Spencer's teacher, Mrs. McClumpsky, gladly gave him a quarter so he could buy a chocolate chip cookie but Spencer was still not happy, not happy at all.

On Thursday, after Spencer got home from preschool, his dad was so busy working on his computer and his mom was so busy rocking Matthew, who was crying yet again, they forgot to watch The Choo-Choo Chippy Show with him.

By Friday, Spencer was mad! That day at preschool he got into a whole heap of trouble. First, he pulled Amber Jones' ponytail during "Alphabet Time", and Mrs. McClumpsky had to put him in the "Time Out" corner.

Next he refused to share the class basketball with his friend, Martin, so Mrs. McClumpsky put him in the "Time Out" corner again. And finally, he kept talking during "Quiet Time". That was the last straw for Mrs. McClumpsky, but instead of putting Spencer in the "Time Out" corner she sat him in a chair beside her desk and asked,

"Spencer Bean, Jr., what is wrong with you this week?" Spencer just shrugged his shoulders.

"You never get into trouble," said Mrs. McClumpsky. "You are one of my Gold Star children!" she said shocked by Spencer's behavior.

Each week Mrs. McClumpsky awarded gold stars to the three children who were the most well behaved, finished their numbers and alphabet, and were as quiet as a mouse during "Quiet Time". Spencer had gotten several gold stars since being in Mrs. McClumpsky's class, well, that was before Matthew came along.

"It's, it's my special gift. It's no fun," whined Spencer.

"Your gift?" asked Mrs. McClumpsky.

"Yes, my mommy and daddy gave me a gift, a baby brotha', and all he does is sleep and cry," he began, "And all my mommy and daddy do are play with him," he said as tears began to run down his face.

"Oh, Spencer, I see," replied Mrs. McClumpsky as she hugged him.

Mrs. McClumpsky had been teaching children Spencer's age for many years and had seen this happen time and time again. Unbeknownst to Spencer, Mrs. McClumpsky decided to call his parents at the end of the school day. She figured once she had a talk with Mr. and Mrs. Bean, they would know just what to do.

When Spencer got home that afternoon, he went right into Matthew's room and sat in his old rocking chair. Matthew was sleeping soundly in his crib.

"Humph," he pouted, "This is my rocking chair and I want it back. You no fun, Baby Brotha'." Spencer's parents quietly walked into Matthew's room to talk to him.

"Junior," said Spencer's mother as she sat in the rocking chair and placed Spencer on her lap. "Daddy and I love you very, very much. You know that, right?"

Spencer looked into his mother's eyes and then looked up at his father's face and replied, "Yes, I know."

"Junior, Mommy and I get busy sometimes but that doesn't mean that we don't love you," his father began, "You are very important to us and we have enough love and attention for you and your baby brother," continued Spencer's father. "And guess, what?"

"What?" asked Spencer curiously.

"Matthew loves you, too. You're his big brother and that makes you very special. Being a big brother is a very important job."
Spencer had not thought of that. He didn't realize that he had an important job and being Matthew's big brother made him special, too.

"I have a job?!" he asked with excitement in his eyes.

"Yes, you do, and you have to set a good example for your baby brother," his mother said. "Now promise us that you're going to behave at preschool for now on, okay?" said Spencer's mother sternly.

"Yes, Mommy, I promise," Spencer said as his parents hugged him tightly.

That evening Spencer's parents took him and his new little brother to Spencer's favorite restaurant, Choo-Choo Chippy's Playhouse, for dinner. He rode Chippy's magical train, played games with his father, and ate pizza until his belly was full. When they got home, Spencer got ready for bed, and fell fast asleep.

In the middle of the night, Spencer was awakened by the sound of a baby whimpering. It was Matthew. His parents were so tired, they had not heard him crying yet so Spencer climbed out of his bed and headed to his little brother's room.

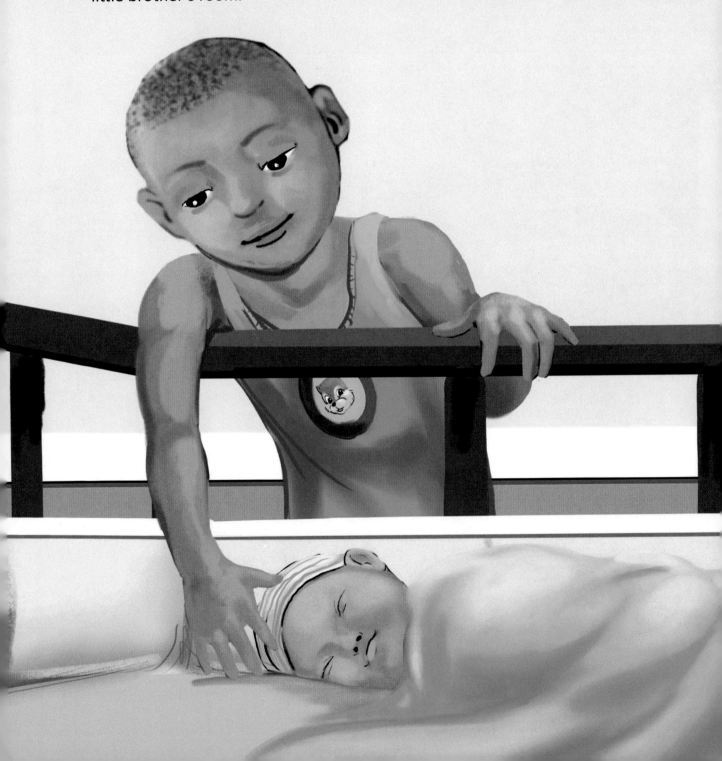

"Don't cry, Baby Brotha'," he whispered as he rubbed the top of Matthew's head. He started singing the Choo-Choo Chippy theme song to him and soon Matthew stopped crying. This made Spencer very happy. With a big smile on his face he looked at Matthew and said,

"I love you, Baby Brotha'! I want you to get bigger and bigger so we can play my Choo-Choo Chippy game and watch the Choo Chippy Show, and..." suddenly Spencer paused, and with a serious voice he continued,

"But not bigger than me. I'm the big brotha'!"

Now Spencer was truly prepared to be a big brother. Well, as prepared as a four-year-old little boy could be.

The
End

Tiffany Elle Burgess is an author and screenwriter. Ms. Burgess earned a Bachelor of Science degree in Biology from Hampton University in 2001 and a Master of Public Health degree from Emory University in 2002. In August 2016, Ms. Burgess released her first children's book, *Skin Like Mine.* The book was well received and has been featured in various publications, including the February 2017 issue of *Essence* magazine. *The Adventures of Junior and Baby Brother: Spencer's Special Gift* is her second children's book. When she is not writing, Ms. Burgess enjoys playing sports and spending quality time with her family and friends.

TeMika Grooms is the illustrator of many children's books including *Nana's Favorite Things* by Dorothy H. Price and *Save the Crash-test Dummies* by Jennifer Swanson. She is intrigued by sequential art, specifically in the form of Children's Literature and Graphic Novels, and the use of powerful storytelling to influence change in society.

Made in the USA
Middletown, DE
28 June 2019